Today in school we studied birds and mammals.
Did you know that Pinkerton and Rose are both mammals?

For homework we're supposed to go on a field trip and identify
ten different birds and mammals. I'll start right here, and
then I'll go to the woods.

Since wild birds and mammals are shy and hard to find,
I'll take Pinkerton and Rose along to help me.

Wait! It's a perfect afternoon for a walk in the woods.
I'll pack a picnic and come too.

Look! My helpers have already spotted the first bird: a scarlet tanager!

Pinkerton! Rose! Come back! We want to identify the birds, not chase them!

Hurry! I think they went this way!

We'll land here. These woods are filled with foxes.

Stake the balloon and post the signs. Our classes
will begin in the next clearing.

Rose! Pinkerton! Where are you?

SILENCE! You are disrupting my class!

Excuse us, but our cat and dog were helping me with my homework, and now they're lost in the woods. Have you seen them?

We can't be bothered with stray animals. We're looking for the noble red fox.

I'd like to see a red fox. He'd be number four on my list. Maybe we could all search together.

Certainly not! This is a private hunting class. You'll have to leave.

Tallyho! A fox! A red fox!

Wait! That's not a fox. Your class is chasing our cat!

Stop shooting, you blockheads, and leash your hounds at once!

I said, STOP SHOOTING!

IDIOTS! This is not a fox! Remember Lesson One!

Excuse me, Doctor Kibble, but there's something rapidly approaching through the trees. Could it be a fox?

It's an invasion from outer space. Run for your lives!

Class, let us leave these fools and return to the hunt.

Never mind them. We'll find a good spot for our picnic,
and then I'll finish my homework.

I'm glad that Pinkerton made friends with the scarlet tanager.

Tallyho! We're hot on the trail!

Well done, class. You have cornered a very rare striped fox.

Excuse me, but he isn't a striped fox.
And I think you'd better not bother him.

Ignore her, class, and surround that fox before it escapes!

Well, this has turned out to be a crazy afternoon walk in the woods. It'll be dark soon, and by the time we clean up the picnic, I'm afraid you won't be able to finish that homework list.

TEN BIRDS AND
MAMMALS I
HAVE SEEN:
1. Rose, A cat.
2. Pinkerton,
   A Great
   Dane
3. The Scarlet
   Tanager.
4. A Striped Skunk.
5.
6.
7.
8.
9.
10.